FROM THE
LIBRARY OF

Klondike & Snow

Published by Roberts Rinehart Publishers

5455 Spine Road, Boulder, Colorado 80301

Published in the UK and Ireland by

Roberts Rinehart Publishers

Trinity House, Charleston Road

Dublin 6, Ireland

Distributed in the U.S. and Canada by

Publishers Group West

Produced and designed by

Betsy Armstrong and Ann W. Douden

BA/AD Books

COVER: *Klondike, with his paw resting on Snow's back, is very protective of his sister.*
CINDY BICKEL

PAGE 1: DAVE KENNY

OPPOSITE: *Klondike looks like he is waving to his friends but actually he is just learning to roll from his back to his belly.*
JOHN AMBROSE

BACK COVER: DAVE KENNY

Klondike & Snow

The Denver Zoo's remarkable story of raising two polar bear cubs

STORY TOLD BY: **David Kenny, V.M.D., Margaret Kenny, Cynthia Bickel, and Dennis R. Roling** from their experiences, observations, and fond recollections.

PHOTOGRAPHY BY: **David & Margaret Kenny, Cynthia and Stephen Bickel, Dennis R. Roling, Bruce Jobe, Bruce & Candy Kane, John & Marion Edwards, Kathy Ogsbury, Jane Wilson, Clayton F. Freiheit, Jimmie L. Eller, John Ambrose, Ann Nagda, Joan Poston, Jackie Zeiler, Ken Neubauer, and Kathy Goede.**

Cindy watches the visitors as the visitors watch Cindy bottle-feed Snow.

Contents

Snow and Klondike behind the hospital pause during their exercise period to suck on Dr. Kenny's hands. BRUCE KANE

Polar bear (Ursus maritimus) CLAYTON FREIHEIT

Adult polar bears also like to play and wrestle in the water. JOHN EDWARDS

Foreword

Polar bears *(Ursus maritimus)* have been cared for in zoological parks for centuries. Denver Zoo's first polar bears were two female cubs, probably sisters, that were mis-named King and Queen. They were received from Point Barrow, Alaska in 1927 and the species has been a continuous feature of our zoo ever since. Velox, an especially popular and endearing polar bear, was retired as a circus performer in 1941 due to failing eyesight. She resided on Bear Mountain until 1960 when she succumbed to the infirmities of old age. Soon after we acquired Sophia and Frank—Sophia survived to the age of thirty-six, which is extraordinary for a polar bear.

When our spacious Northern Shores exhibit was opened in 1987 we obtained six young polar bears, all born in other U.S. zoos, to populate the new area. Denver Zoo had successfully raised polar bear cubs on two separate occasions in 1974 and 1977; we hoped for similar good fortune when, on the morning of November 6, 1994, two newborn polar bear cubs were discovered abandoned by their mother, Ulu.

This is their remarkable story, and we are fortunate to be able to write it. But it is also a chronicle of the dedication, hard work, frustration, and anxiety that are typically all part of the foster rearing of any delicate newborn animal.

The authors of this book have all been intimately involved in our Herculean efforts to raise Klondike and Snow to strong, healthy independence and are uniquely qualified to share their experience in this book.

Clayton F. Freiheit
Director,
Denver Zoological Gardens

The cubs seemed to be as interested in the media as the media was in their story. JANE WILSON

TOP: *Klondike at 2 months showing his "devil face," scowling at a close-up.* BOTTOM: *One month later, Klondike buries his face in the snow, posing readily.*

DAVE KENNY

Preface

The birth of polar bears in captivity is not an unusual occurrence. But, for the Denver Zoo, the birth of Klondike and Snow on November 6, 1994 was to become an event unlike any other in the Zoo's recent history. Rejected by their natural mother, Klondike and Snow were taken to the zoo hospital and immediately embraced by the staff, visitors, and the media. For the first three months of their lives they were taken home at night by their designated foster "parents" for intensive round-the-clock care.

When the cubs were strong enough to stay in the zoo's nursery through the night, their "parents" went through bear withdrawal—six people had been their mother and father, held them, bathed them, cleaned up after them, watched them grow, loved them, and let them go.

How could two such tiny and frail animals capture the hearts of so many people? This chronicle of their first five months of life and the outstanding collection of photographs capture their progress from birth (weighing barely one pound and screaming) to strong, agile cubs, and the joy and triumph of the many people who helped to raise them.

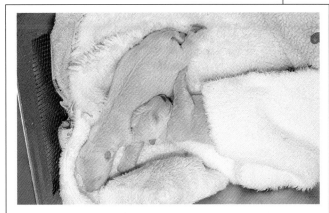

From one-pound frail babies to agile cubs.

(TOP) CINDY BICKEL (BOTTOM) JOHN EDWARDS

A reluctant Klondike is returned to the nursery after a play session in the snow. JOHN AMBROSE

Acknowledgments

The story of Klondike and Snow would never have been told if it were not for the extraordinary efforts of many people. We are extremely grateful to Margaret Kenny for proposing we write this book and then contributing as an author. We also thank Clayton Freiheit, Director, Angela Baier, Marketing Director, and Elaine Anderson, Ph.D., Denver Museum of Natural History, for editing the manuscript prior to submission. When the cubs went home each night three non-zoo recruits shared duties as surrogate parents: Margaret Kenny, Steve Bickel, and Bruce Jobe spent many sleepless nights caring for the babies.

Many medical consultants assisted with the care of our cubs by generously contributing their time and expertise. Radiology, Jimmie L. Eller, M.D.; Ultrasonography, staff from the Children's Hospital and Linda J. Konde, D.V.M., Dip., A.C.V.R.; Pediatric Gastroenterology, Ronald J. Sokol, M.D.; Surgery,

Robert A. Taylor, D.V.M., Dip. A.C.V.S.; Dentistry, Peter Emily, D.D.S., Dip., A.V.D.C.; Nutrition, Nancy A. Irlbeck, Ph.D., Wendy S. Graffam; Physical Therapy, Merry N. Lester, P.T., O.C.S; Lactational Therapist, Gay Klein.

In addition, we are indebted to the Denver Zoo's hospital staff and docents. These behind-the-scenes people performed the day-in, day-out thankless chores that were necessary for such an intensive effort to succeed. Docent Russ Young deserves special mention for the many long hours he spent outside the nursery educating the public on his favorite animal, the polar bear. Zoo docents and security staff spent many hours answering questions and keeping order while visitors patiently waited for an opportunity to see the bears. The Zoo's hospital, marketing, and administrative staff answered countless phone calls from the public concerning the bears. We are very thankful to Gary Aguirre for finding the cubs so promptly and the Animal Department for sharing their expertise and advice on hand-raising the cubs. The Denver metro and Front Range media deserve our thanks for the professional and sensitive manner in which they handled the bears' story.

Kathy Ogsbury, one of the many hospital volunteers who put in long hours helping raise the cubs, holding Klondike at 4 weeks old. JOHN EDWARDS

Klondike and Snow's parents, Olaf and Ulu, also are never found far apart, often seen sleeping and playing together.

DAVE KENNY

BOTTOM: MARION EDWARDS

The First Day

The morning of November 6, 1994 started as any other Sunday on call. Dr. Kenny, senior veterinarian for the Denver Zoo, was out in the park seeing patients and performing treatments. Gary Aguirre, the polar bear keeper, had arrived at Northern Shores and was inspecting his animals. He thought he heard a strange soft crying. Ulu, who had been bred the previous year by Olaf, was closed into a cubbing den but also had access to a hallway. A camera mounted in the den permitted keepers to observe the bear in the den or the hallway

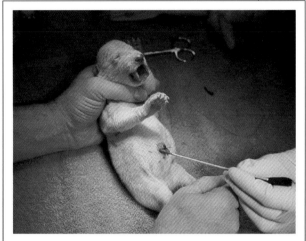

Klondike just a few hours old having his umbilicus treated to prevent infection. CINDY BICKEL

from a monitor in the kitchen without disturbing her. Gary checked the monitor and saw two small white objects in the hallway. He immediately recognized that the cries were from newborn polar bears cubs and that they were alive. It was difficult for Gary to express the excitement and exhilaration he felt to see the first live babies from a group of animals he had been taking care of for several years. The same emotions filled him as when his own first child was born.

This excitement quickly changed to concern when he realized the cubs, a male and a female, were extremely chilled and their short lives were ebbing away. Their inexperienced mother had abandoned them. At 8:30 A.M. came a radio call that would change our lives and the zoo for the next several months and perhaps forever. The cubs were on their way to the hospital. They were bundled in blankets and transported in a golf cart with the assistance of the area supervisor, Vickie Kunter.

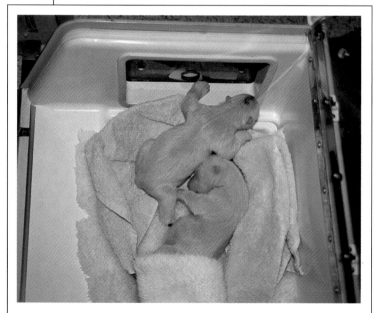

At birth, the cubs were placed in an incubator, the temperature set at 90 ° F.

DAVE KENNY

It is not unusual for polar bears to give birth in captivity, but it is unusual to successfully hand-raise cubs that have been abandoned. Such cubs are often found severely chilled (dependent on their mothers at this stage for warmth) or they have been traumatized. A mother that is stressed or nervous after giving birth may injure or even kill her cubs.

Denny Roling, hospital keeper on duty for the weekend, heard the radio call that the cubs were on their way to the hospital. Questions raced through his mind: *What are they like? How big are they? What shape are they in? What do I need to get ready?* Cindy Bickel, a hospital keeper with experience hand-raising many orphaned babies at the Denver Zoo, was called and quickly came in on her day off.

Upon arrival at the hospital the cubs were quickly weighed and placed in a human infant incubator. They weighed 1 $\frac{1}{4}$ pounds, and just fit into the palm of a human hand. They were softly vocalizing. The cubs had pink skin and were covered with very fine white hair. Their heads seemed disproportionately larger than their bodies. But even these enormous heads were not sufficiently large enough to house their gigantic tongues. The tips of their pink tongues could often be seen protruding from their mouths while at rest.

Newborn polar bear cubs have pink skin and are covered with fine white hair.
CINDY BICKEL

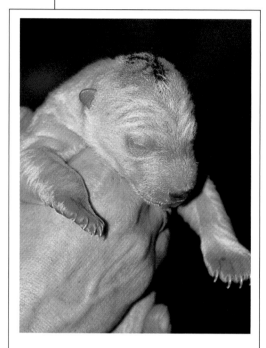

Klondike had a 3-inch laceration on the top of his head which had to be sutured. JOHN EDWARDS

Their temperatures at 9:00 A.M. would not register on a thermometer and we were not able to get a temperature reading until noon that first day. They had not nursed and were weak and barely moving. In addition, the male cub had a three-inch laceration on the top of his head extending through to the skull. Gary named the female Snow and the male Klondike. How could such tiny feeble creatures mature into the largest terrestrial carnivores of the Arctic?

The primary objective at this point was to raise their core body temperatures. The incubator was set at 86°F. The umbilical cords were sutured and removed close to the body and the stumps treated with tincture of iodine to prevent infection. As the cubs began to warm, their vocalizations became more intense, indicating that they were becoming stronger and were now hungry.

Since the cubs had not nursed from their mother, they did not receive the maternal antibodies in that first milk, known as colostrum, which could be critical in protecting these infants from infections. As an alternative, we tube-fed both cubs with blood serum collected from their mother and frozen during a previous examination. The cubs would be tube-fed until they gained strength because we were concerned that they might aspirate milk into their lungs and die from pneumonia. This is not an uncommon complication when hand-raising baby animals. The cubs were also fed a human electrolyte solution while we gathered the ingredients to try to make an artificial polar bear milk.

How do you make polar bear milk anyway? A discussion was held later that morning at the zoo hospital with the general curator, senior veterinarian, and the two hospital keepers. We gathered all the available literature on the subject from the zoo library and a recent publication sponsored by the American Zoo and Aquarium Association on the hand-rearing of zoo animal infants, including a chapter on bears. The selected diet consisted of

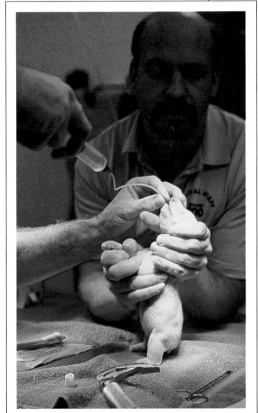

The cubs were too weak to nurse for the first three days so they were tube-fed until they gained strength. CINDY BICKEL

Esbilac®, a puppy milk replacer, half-and-half, and several vitamin and mineral supplements. Both cubs were fed this formula by stomach tube the first day.

How do you make polar bear milk anyway?

The next questions were: how and by whom would the cubs be cared for at night, and would the little bears be alive tomorrow?

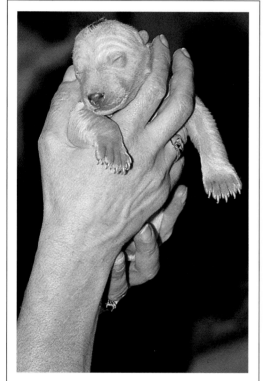

Klondike, just a few hours old, so small that he fit in the palm of Cindy's hand. JOHN EDWARDS

The cubs liked to snuggle together in the incubator, sleeping on fleece that simulated a mother's fur. DAVE KENNY

Would the little bears be alive tomorrow?

With their bellies full of milk, the cubs are ready to nap. CINDY BICKEL

Home Alone

When Snow and Klondike first came to the zoo hospital there was very little information on how to raise baby polar bears. With the birth of any animal there are procedures to be followed from preparation of a holding area, to feeding, to treatment if necessary. Given the cubs' fragile condition, it quickly became obvious that intensive round-the-clock care would be necessary to ensure their survival. Who better to care for them than the zoo vet and hospital staff? Dr. Dave Kenny, Cindy Bickel, and Denny Roling had the honor of being selected as Klondike and Snow's surrogate parents. They would, in three-night intervals, take the bears home and administer to their needs from 5:00 P.M., after the zoo closed, until 8:00 A.M. the following morning. Each of them had been on baby duty before. But, except for Cindy who had been a surrogate mother to many other Denver Zoo newborns, no one anticipated to what lengths that job would go. So Cindy was assigned the awesome responsibility of taking the bear cubs home that first night.

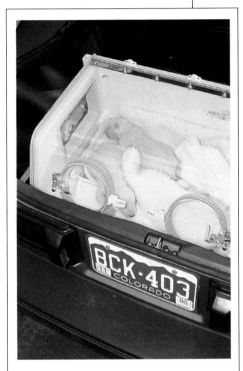

The cubs are loaded in a warm incubator and then into Cindy's car for the trip home.
CINDY BICKEL

At two months, Klondike and Snow cuddle—one of the few moments they both slept at the same time. Even when the cubs slept, one of their surrogate parents watched over them. CINDY BICKEL

For the next three months, night and morning, the bears were transported in a metal box lined with towels and soft fleece material to protect and keep them warm on their journey through Denver traffic. On one such trip, Dr. Kenny stopped at a donut shop on his way back to the zoo with his precious cargo on board. He returned to his car with coffee and donut in hand to find two Denver police officers peering suspiciously into the back seat. Dave explained his mission and set off, leaving two very surprised faces in the parking lot.

Special gear needed for their care was piled into trunks every night—a portable incubator, a plastic garbage bag overstuffed with towels, many small bottles of formula, and a red tackle box filled with various medical supplies. It took several people to load all the supplies each evening.

The first night each "parent" took Klondike and Snow home, reactions from spouses and roommates ranged from excitement to reserve. They were among only a handful of people who had ever before been this close to infant polar bears. This was an awesome responsibility. Would they be capable of handling such a demanding job? Initial emotions were soon replaced by methodical preparations for the night. Rooms were arranged to enable close surveillance of the babies in their incubator. While the first bottles were being warmed, Klondike and Snow were transferred to the incubator and a comfortable temperature was set. The human parents could finally relax after a sometimes stressful drive home from the zoo. They reported that, at times, the bears' screams were so intense they could barely hear the traffic.

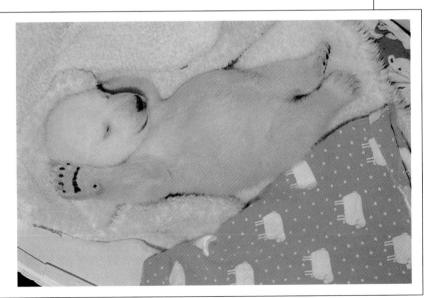

Snow in her bassinet sleeping on her back.
CINDY BICKEL

Meg plays with the cubs while the bottles warm on the stove. DAVE KENNY

First feedings were usually shared events with the more experienced person feeding Klondike, a frantic feeder, who was still recuperating from his wounds suffered at birth. Every two hours, starting at 7:30 P.M., they would be fed, stimulated with a damp cloth to urinate and defecate, and put to bed. Shared duties became the norm, but even with the best laid plans, one person usually took over the hectic late-night and early-morning feedings. As with all babies, they had to be watched constantly until they fell asleep. Invariably, one would be more fussy, and when finally calmed down, the other would start—as if they knew how to get attention.

Sometimes, in the middle of the night, the bears would wake up and cry. Giving them a finger to suck on would keep them quiet. Cindy found that sleeping next to the incubator made it easy to reach the babies through the portals and use her finger as a pacifier that was eagerly taken by both Klondike and Snow. Then Cindy could rest her head on the top of the incubator and try to catnap before the next bout of crying began.

Their unusually large tongues had the most amazing sucking power, much like the concentrated pull from the end of a vacuum cleaner attachment. After a few days the cubs started emitting sounds that resembled a cat purring loudly or a small motor running, or a toy machine gun! It was very soothing for both surrogate parents and cub to hear this noise. This sound, or chortling, indicated that the cubs were quite content.

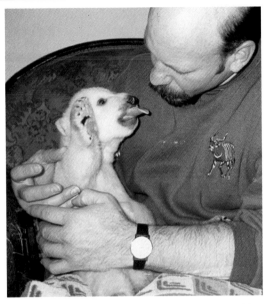

As with all babies, the cubs liked it when we blew softly in their face. They responded by extending their enormous tongues. BRUCE JOBE

Those first nights were sleepless, worrisome times. Put the babies in the incubator, set up the sleeping quarters, adjust the temperature, eat dinner, warm their milk, feed them, wipe their bottom with a damp cloth, put them back in the incubator, clean and sterilize the bottles, do the laundry, and try to relax until the next feeding. Getting through the night with very little sleep and having to focus on these fragile, dependent babies took its toll. But each morning when Klondike and Snow headed back to the zoo, a hot shower and the knowledge that they were still OK was enough to get their adopted parents all set for the day. That was the routine in the first few weeks.

After their screams subsided and they stopped fussing, the cubs slept soundly, but not for more than 15 minutes at a time.

CINDY BICKEL

When the cubs' size prohibited them from sleeping together in the incubator, Denny donated a white portable bassinet. Normally that was Snow's bed, which allowed her some peace and quiet from an ever-pawing brother. Klondike stayed in the incubator, with the cover now left open. After about two weeks, the nighttime parents were discovering ways to cope with the screams. Denny had the most luck with using a sleeping bag and letting them crawl inside to simulate a real "den." In the beginning this worked well to create a cozy and warm environment, but as they grew and their fur thickened, warm rooms made them uncomfortable. So the heat was turned down.

Being held was not one of their favorite pastimes, especially in the beginning. And they *hated* getting a bath. Because the formula was high in fat, their feces were very oily. If we didn't catch them going to the bathroom, it would wind up on them. Imagine yellow-colored lard being ground into white fur—impossible to just rub off. So, run to the kitchen, fill the sink with warm water, get plenty of towels and work fast—work up a lather, with mild soap on your hands, and clean their bottoms, all the while trying to ignore their ear-splitting screams and avoid being bitten. Oddly enough, after a quick cleaning and rub with a towel, their screams stopped when the warm air of a hair dryer swept over their faces. Noise and all, they liked it!

When the cubs outgrew their "enclosures" (incubator and bassinet), we gave them a larger space by barricading a section of a room where they could explore. The sleeping bags, now christened with bear droppings, quickly became bear property and were given up for their exclusive use. When Cindy took her sleeping

A little disheveled, Meg and Dave play with the cubs after a 2 A.M. feeding.

DAVE KENNY

While playing with Klondike, Bruce got a little too close and was grabbed by the nose—ouch! DENNY ROLING

bag back to the bears after three months, they immediately recognized the scent, jumped on top, and contentedly fell asleep.

It was more difficult to jump over barricades in the never-ending feeding ritual but the bonus was that the cubs had become playful. Now, instead of crying constantly, they were always on the move. They enjoyed being touched and cuddled and would lie on their backs to have their tummies rubbed. Klondike especially liked this and would let us blow on his face and kiss his stomach—all the things you do with small children. Bruce Jobe discovered, too late one night, that as part of their maturing, the cubs were developing quick reflexes. While bending over the baby to snuggle close, Klondike bit the end of his nose. Ouch! Those teeth were really starting to hurt. It was the best part of caring for them. Yes, the house smelled like—what was it??—cod liver oil. The basement was a mess, and we knew that every third night there wouldn't be much sleep, but it was a job everyone envied.

Things usually went smoothly and, save for very tiring nights, the bears progressed. Each parent had their own touch and all felt a well-deserved sense of pride in helping Klondike and Snow mature into rambunctious cubs. There were moments for all of us when one or both of the bears caused us to PANIC. Just before a 2 A.M. feeding, Klondike stuck his face in a bowl of water placed on the floor. He must have thought he could breathe under water. He started to turn blue but was too panicked to pull his head out of the bowl. We quickly extricated him from what was both a comical and life threatening situation. Klondike snorted and fell back, dazed and confused, and began what sounded like coughing. Meg Kenny started screaming for Dave, fearful that Klondike had aspirated water into his lungs. The cub immediately became lethargic, but Dave took one look, listened to his chest, and said to wait until morning. Meg took up vigil by his side, not sleeping, listening to his breathing. Fortunately by morning he was just fine.

After a play-filled day, the cubs enjoy cooling down by napping on a slab of ice. CINDY BICKEL

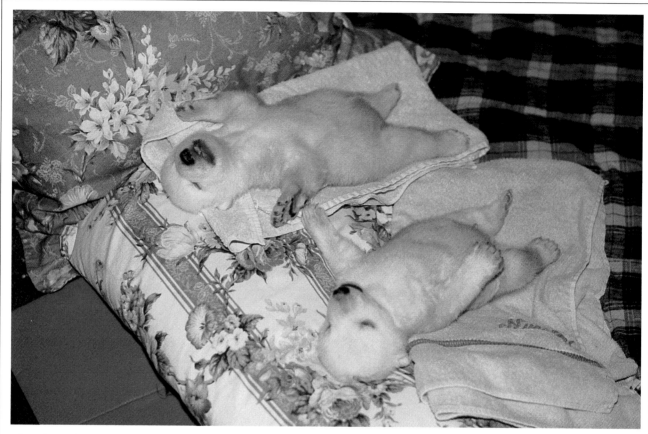

The cubs quickly outgrew the incubator and preferred sleeping on Cindy's sleeping bag and pillow. CINDY BICKEL

The sleeping bags, now christened with bear droppings,
quickly became bear property.

Steve looks forward to his chance to play with the cubs.

CINDY BICKEL

Steve uses his own special touch to pacify two fussy cubs.

CINDY BICKEL

*Things usually went
smoothly.*

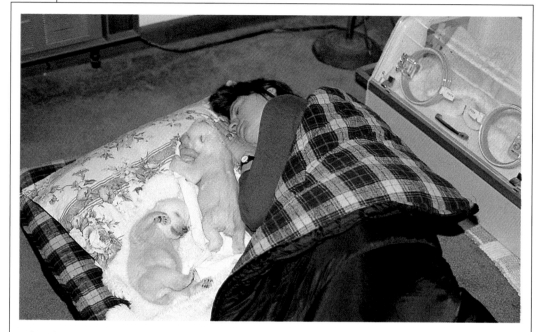

When they outgrew their incubator and bassinet, their "territory" was expanded. STEVE BICKEL

When Cindy took her sleeping bag back to the bears after three months, they immediately recognized the scent, jumped on top and fell contentedly asleep.

While Klondike sleeps, Denny talks to a friend in Holland who just saw our "ice bears" on television. BRUCE JOBE

They would lie on their backs to have their tummies rubbed.

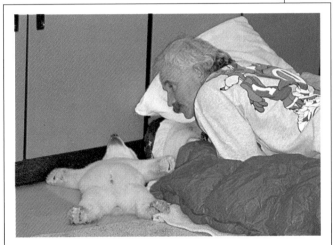

Dr. Kenny says, "If you told me I would be spending hours watching a polar bear cub sleep, I would have said you were crazy!" MEG KENNY

Cindy is learning that two growing polar bear cubs are quite the armful. STEVE BICKEL

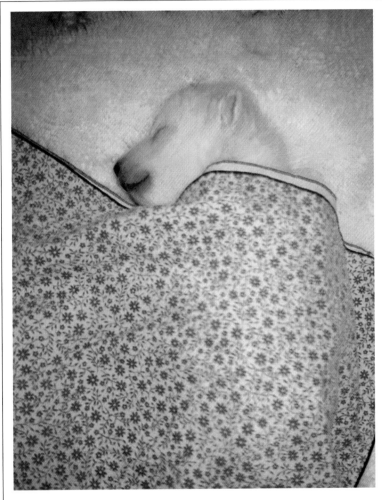

Snow is tucked in for the night. CINDY BICKEL

Klondike snoozes on the ice pack. CANDY KANE

The Fight for Survival

We noticed in the first few days that Klondike did not nurse as well as his sister, Snow. Fortunately a lactational therapist was in the public viewing area of the nursery watching the cubs. Cindy was out in the nursery lobby and an important conversation transpired. It seems that human infants who have suffered head trauma can also have trouble nursing. The remedy is to slip your pinky along the lower jaw and pull it down while the baby is nursing. This helps the tongue to protrude further, and some infants will nurse more effectively. Klondike's nursing improved immediately.

When the cubs were one week old we noted that they were having trouble with bloating, Klondike being more severely affected. This reached a critical stage when Cindy had the cubs at home—she frantically called Dr. Kenny to report that Klondike was bloated, lethargic, and refusing to nurse. His soft plaintiff cries were heart-wrenching. He was immediately taken off milk and tube-fed with a human infant electrolyte formula to prevent dehydration, and given additional fluids subcutaneously. This reduced the bloat, he became more

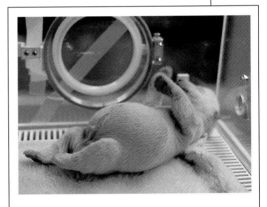

Klondike with a polar bear-sized belly ache.
CINDY BICKEL

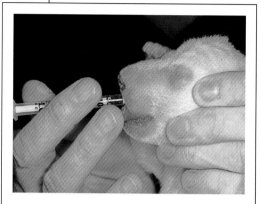

Polar bear cub being treated for internal parasites.

DAVE KENNY

active, and towards morning, was interested in nursing. Blood samples were taken the next day but were unremarkable.

One possibility adversely affecting the cubs' health was that captive polar bears are routinely afflicted with roundworms, an internal parasite. In addition to the bloating, both cubs would routinely have a small amount of blood in their stools which could be a sign of migrating parasites. After the cubs were treated orally for parasites, the bloody stools ceased but the bloating continued.

The Denver Zoo is quite fortunate in having many specialists willing to donate their time consulting on our difficult cases. They stepped forward as soon as it was learned that the cubs were in trouble. We were concerned that the problem might be an obstruction in the gastrointestinal tract. A radiographic study was conducted to evaluate the cubs for an obstruction and was interpreted by a radiologist. Barium was administered to the cubs through a stomach tube and sequential radiographs were taken to follow the progress of the dye. We performed the procedure on both cubs so we could use one for comparison. The barium passed all the way through the digestive tract, eliminating the possibility of a complete obstruction. A specialist in pediatric gastroenterology from the Denver Children's Hospital examined the cubs and recommended that both be ultrasounded. Two ultrasonography exams did not reveal any abnormalities. In desperation we even considered doing exploratory abdominal surgery on Klondike.

Perhaps the problem was nutritional. We received and followed advice to switch from cod liver oil to safflower oil to see if that would correct the bloating problem; and indeed, it stopped. The cubs were now seventeen days old.

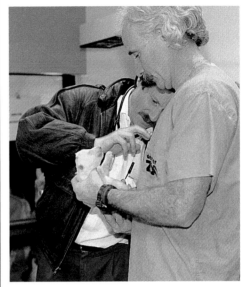

Dr. Sokol, a pediatric gastroenterologist from Children's Hospital in Denver, examines Klondike at the zoo. CINDY BICKEL

Snow now started to fail, becoming more lethargic and crying a lot. Again, both cubs were radiographed and to our dismay both cubs had many fractured bones. Only sixteen days after changing oils, when the cubs were thirty-three days old, they had developed rickets. Rickets is usually caused by inadequate levels of vitamin D_3, a vitamin necessary for the absorption of calcium and phosphorus from the intestine. Humans and animals make vitamin D_3 by exposure to the ultraviolet wavelength from sunlight. If you live indoors or in a snow cave, adequate levels of vitamin D_3 need to be obtained from your diet. We didn't know what the necessary minimum level of dietary vitamin D_3 was for polar

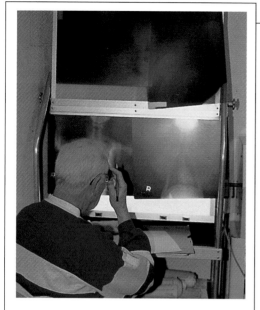

Dr. Jimmie Eller reviews the cubs' radiographs during their episode with rickets. DAVE KENNY

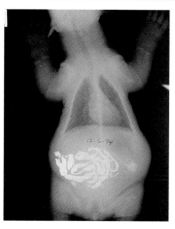

Radiograph of a barium dye study on a polar bear cub.

JIMMIE ELLER

bear cubs. Normally the mother takes care of this for the cubs. Calcium and phosphorus are essential for the formation of healthy bones. This is more critical in a rapidly growing animal.

It is difficult to describe how distraught we felt at this time. Although we manipulated and changed the cubs' diet with the best of intentions, we could not help feeling guilty. Did we discover the problem early enough and could we reverse the damage?

In retrospect we believe Snow was more profoundly affected by the rickets because at the time she was growing more rapidly than Klondike. The rapidity of the disease process was still amazing. The cubs were immediately given an injection of vitamin D_3, the safflower oil removed and replaced with cod liver oil, and extra calcium added to the milk formula. Follow-up radiographs a week later showed that the tiny fractured limbs had already begun to heal.

In order to do everything possible to help rehabilitate Snow we enlisted the services of a physical therapist. She had previous experience working with animal patients at a local veterinary practice. We developed a set of exercises to do each day with Snow. After each feeding it was time for aerobics—flex those legs one-two-three, work those thighs one-two-three. Needless to say, Snow objected to doing forced aerobics and would try to bite her "tormentor."

Periodic radiographic evaluations were performed until the cubs were 122 days old. They showed that the only remaining abnormality was a bowing in Snow's right femur, the bone that goes from the hip to the knee. This remaining affected bone shows evidence that it is continuing to remodel and could eventually become completely normal.

The final dietary adjustment we made was to increase the percentage of Esbilac® and decrease the half-and-half. It did not seem that our cubs were gaining weight fast enough when compared to weights given in the literature of a few other hand-raised cubs. Although our diet was based on a milk analysis from a polar bear, others have raised cubs on straight Esbilac® and no half-and-half. The half-

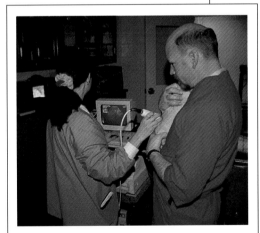

Radiologist Dr. Linda Konde ultrasounding a polar bear cub. DAVE KENNY

and-half was added to imitate the high fat content found in polar bear milk. Unfortunately, we didn't know how nutritionally available the nutrients from our fabricated diet were to a polar bear cub. We theorized the slow growth was due to a need for more protein. We settled on a formula of 60 percent Esbilac® and 40 percent half-and-half. After this change the cubs started to gain weight rapidly and have been doing well ever since.

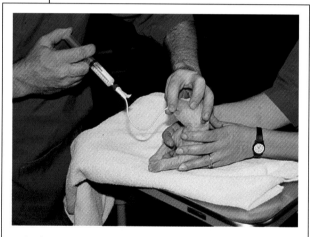

Tube feeding was often a two-person job. DAVE KENNY

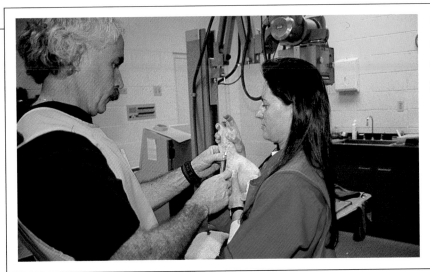

Periodic blood samples were taken to track the cubs' health status.
JOAN POSTON

We didn't know how nutritionally available the nutrients from our fabricated diet were to a polar bear cub.

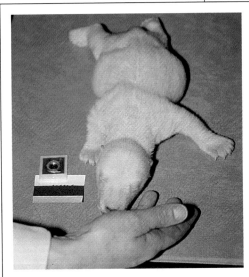

Cub being pacified prior to a radiographic examination. DAVE KENNY

Initially, Snow (right) was growing and developing much faster than her brother Klondike (left).

STEVE BICKEL

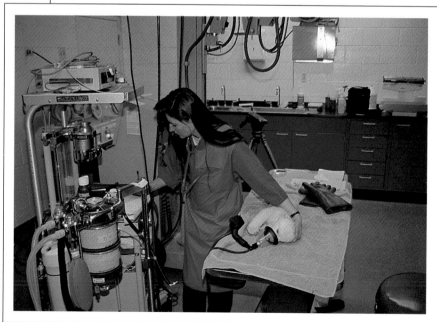

Cindy monitors anesthesia during a physical exam on a cub.

DAVE KENNY

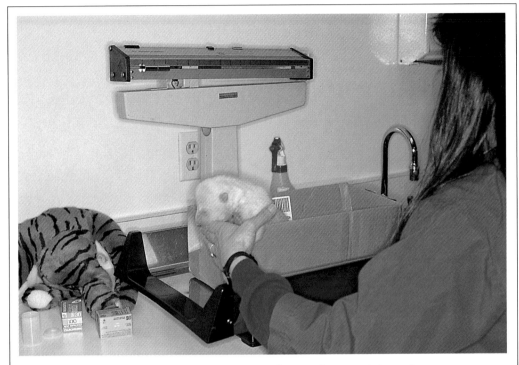

While the cubs were small, we weighed them by putting them in a box on an infant scale. DAVE KENNY

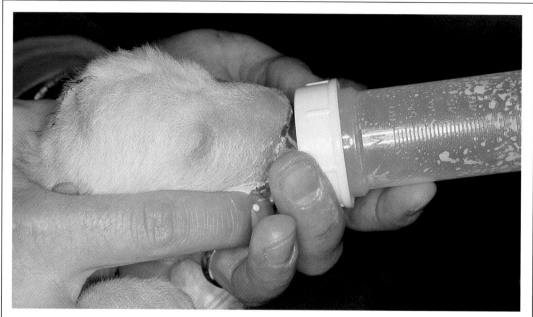

Klondike drains every last drop of his bottle. DAVE KENNY

After this change the cubs started to gain weight
rapidly and have been doing well ever since.

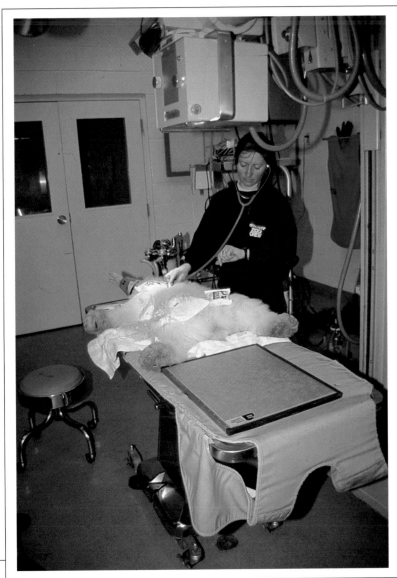

As the cubs grew, anesthesia and radiography became greater challenges. Cindy monitors Klondike at four months.

DAVE KENNY

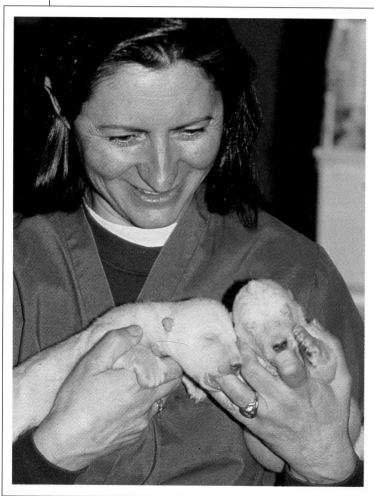

Cindy pacifies the three-week-old cubs at once by letting them suck on her fingers.

JOHN EDWARDS

Growing Up a Polar Bear

It was mind-boggling to see how quickly the cubs grew from week to week. The growth and development of a polar bear cub was something completely outside our life experience. When we laid one of the cubs beside an adult male polar bear skull, the skull dwarfed the cub. A polar bear starts as a one-pound, pink-skinned baby covered with very fine fur. A larger cub would put a tremendous drain on its mother who has not eaten for months and will not eat for another two to three months. The incredible rate of weight gain for a polar bear cub illustrates another important feature of the species—sexual dimorphism. In the case of the polar bear, adult males are two to three times larger than females. Males may range from 650 to 1700 pounds, and females 330 to 660 pounds. We could see this as Klondike became larger and heavier than his sister. We also charted some of the significant events in the lives of Klondike and Snow.

We gave Klondike and Snow slabs of ice to simulate life in the Arctic. JOHN EDWARDS

Development of Klondike and Snow

Date of Birth 11/06/94

	Klondike	Snow
Sex	Male	Female
Birth weight	1.25 lbs	1.25 lbs
Eyes open	33 days	34 days
Teething	39 days	39 days
Standing	80 days	99 days
Walking	89 days	106 days

Three and a half year old Greg Goede, playing with a truck, gains the interest of the curious cubs. At five months old, the bears outweigh their visitor. KATHY GOEDE

During their first few days of life, polar bear cubs are extremely dependent upon their mother for warmth. We confirmed this with our own experience in hand-raising Klondike and Snow. Initially the cubs seemed to be comfortable in the incubator set at 90°F. After about ten days they developed a thick luxurious coat of hair and became very heat sensitive. They quickly started to pant when overheated. As the weeks and months passed, we found they liked the environmental temperature to be less than 70°F. After playing, they particularly enjoyed cooling off by lying on a large slab of ice.

Polar bear cubs are totally dependent upon their mothers for their survival for two to three years. Mothers that emerge from their snow dens with twins or triplets are often seen a year later with a single cub. Cub mortality is apparently high. Finding enough food for a large carnivore in the Arctic and avoiding other hungry bears is a constant struggle.

The feeding program underwent dramatic changes as the cubs developed. We started with tube-feeding every two hours. This technique is pretty scary on an animal that can fit in the palm of your hand. We progressed to bottle-feeding every two, then three, and finally every four hours. After the cubs learned to stand we offered them milk in bowls. It took

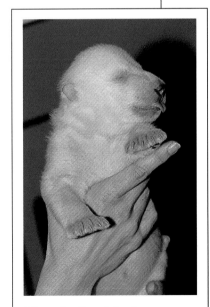

We can hardly wait for them to open their eyes. JOHN EDWARDS

Before the cubs could stand, we needed to support them during bottle feeding—a task that hospital volunteer Candy Kane gladly accepted.

KATHY OGSBURY

them a while to understand they should lap the milk up with their tongues, not snort it up through their noses. Finally, they learned to eat and enjoy canned dog food, dry bear biscuits, and their favorite, trout fillets; but who wouldn't?

Many people have asked if the cubs cared for each other. For a while we thought that they just tolerated one another. Quite often they would be seen sleeping at opposite ends of the nursery. One afternoon, Snow became quite ill with vomiting and explosive diarrhea. She was extremely lethargic; she looked like she might die. Because Klondike kept pawing and climbing on her, wanting to play, we put Snow in a plexiglass whelping box in the nursery so she could sleep unmolested. Klondike parked himself against the plexiglass front and did not leave until she recovered and came out of the box. When we arrived each morning, the cubs were sleeping in a heap and we were unable to distinguish where one began and the other ended.

As the cubs developed, one of the first changes in their mobility was their learning how to roll over and sleep on their backs. However, after they woke they could not roll back on their bellies. They screamed at the top of their lungs, and soon learned that someone would come and roll them back over. A polar bear cub sleeping on its back is a sight to behold. It's like watching dad asleep snoring on the couch.

For the first month the cubs' eyes were closed. When their eyes first opened and started to focus, we all wondered what their initial image of the world around them would be. What would they think of the strange looking creatures who were taking care of them?

The cubs grew rapidly on the new milk diet. When nursing, a cub's tongue surrounds the nipple and forces it against the hard palate, producing an enormous amount of suction. The nipples we used had to have extremely small holes to prevent the cubs from swallowing the milk too rapidly and aspirating it into their lungs. Between feedings we frequently inserted a pinky or index finger into their mouths to pacify them. We were impressed with how far down the back of the mouth the cubs took the finger. This procedure became

At three and a half months, Snow has mastered the art of bottle feeding without assistance. DAVE KENNY

Snow plays her favorite game of peek-a-boo. KATHY OGSBURY

more painful after the cubs began teething.

Play is an important feature of any infant's early life. Free-ranging polar bear adults and cubs have been seen playing. Large males have even been seen playing with sled dogs chained outside in Churchill, Manitoba. It was no different for Klondike and Snow. They could spend hours chasing each other around the nursery or wrestling. They also liked to play tug-of-war with their favorite blanket. When they were little, they enjoyed playing peek-a-boo with Cindy and a blanket. We wrestled with them until their playful nips seemed to penetrate even the thickest of garments.

One of the major milestones for the cubs, and for those caring for them, was when they first learned to stand and then walk. For two and a half months they looked like living bearskin rugs. They would lie flat on their bellies with their legs stretched out to the side. One day we noticed that Klondike was using his nose as a brace to rise up on all fours, with his pendulous baby belly just off the ground for a few moments. He looked like a white furry pentapod. He then started to use one of the ledges in the nursery to brace himself and scoot along the ledge to the delight of the zoo visitors. It is impossible to describe the excitement and exhilaration we felt the day he stood for the first time. Just a few days later he took his first few wobbly steps. We were both proud and relieved.

Dr. Kenny helps Snow with her first few steps.
MEG KENNY

Snow was a different story. Since she was more severely affected by rickets, we wondered if she would ever be able to stand and walk. While Klondike was walking and stumbling around the room Snow would scoot around on her belly crying, unable to keep up with him. Then, three weeks after her brother took his first feeble steps, Snow suddenly rose up on all four legs for just a second. We breathed a collective sigh of relief and then spread the news to anyone who would listen. It would be only a matter of days before Snow was walking too.

Klondike goes for a walk in the zoo in his harness; ducks and bunnies beware! CANDY KANE

After they learned to walk, we took them outside for an exercise period each morning and late afternoon when the zoo was closed. They particularly enjoyed it when there was snow on the ground. They loved to bury their heads in the snow and burrow like a mole. They would also roll around in the snow on their backs. Every bush and tree had to be investigated. The resident geese, peafowl, and rabbits decided to move to other parts of the zoo. Bears have a lumbering style of walking but can be quite agile and graceful when running. Playing and running with the cubs is a cherished memory for all of us. Our next task was to teach the cubs to swim. *Do* you teach polar bears to swim? Is that a behavior they innately know? Free-ranging polar bears are powerful swimmers. Some have been seen miles out at sea. Even cubs that have recently emerged from the den will swim with their mothers between ice floes. In fact, the United States considers them marine mammals and affords them protection under the Marine Mammal Act.

We already knew Klondike and Snow were not very fond of their Friday night bath, so would they enjoy swimming? First we purchased a toddler's plastic wading pool. Klondike quickly learned to jump in and out of the pool chasing anything that moved. Snow draped herself over the edge but was reluctant to get in and splash with her brother.

Since the cubs were too small to go immediately to our Northern Shores exhibit and the large polar bear pool, it was decided to move them to a modified

A toddler's wading pool gave the cubs their first experience with water. JOHN EDWARDS

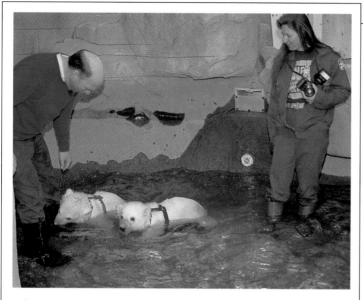

After graduating to a deeper pool, the cubs receive swimming lessons from Denny and Cindy. DAVE KENNY

penguin exhibit on an interim basis. The penguins were relocated before the bears arrived. This exhibit has a large concrete pool and was considered an excellent place for the cubs to sharpen their swimming skills. Each morning before the zoo opened, we harnessed the bears and walked them to the pool. Donning wet suits, we entered the pool with the cubs not far behind. Swimming came naturally for them. The only difference we noted was that initially they were paddling with all four legs. The adults power themselves with their front legs, their hind legs trail outstretched behind. The cubs were very buoyant, bobbing up and down like apples. What a special feeling it was to float in the pool with two polar bear cubs in tow.

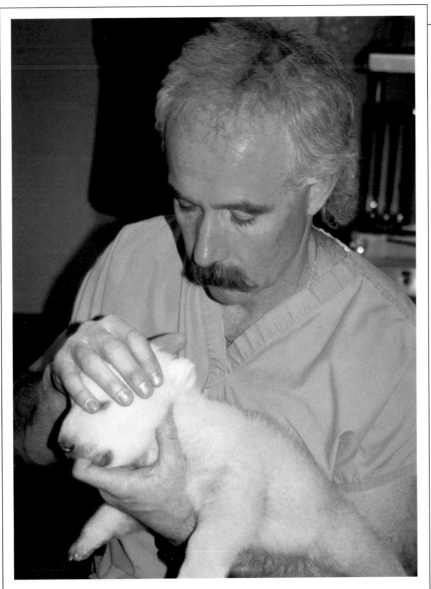

Dr. Kenny comforts Snow as she recovers from anesthesia. JIMMIE ELLER

Klondike enjoys having the back of his neck scratched.

JOHN EDWARDS

Growing up in the nursery.

Klondike's eyes opening for the first time, he sees the people who have been feeding and caring for him.

DAVE KENNY

Like most infants, polar bear cubs spend most of their time sleeping.

KATHY OGSBURY

While teething, Snow enjoyed having her gums massaged.

KATHY OGSBURY

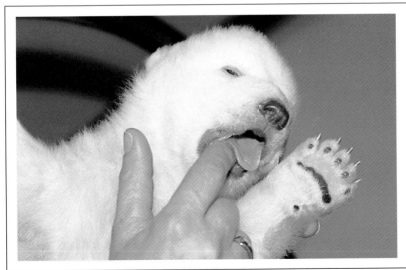

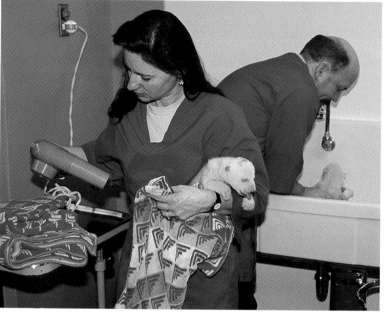

The cubs' screams were ear-splitting when bath time arrived but stopped when the warm air of the hair dryer swept over their faces. **DAVE** KENNY

Dreaded baths . . . except for that hair dryer.

Simple chew toys were needed to exercise a mouth full of new teeth.

KATHY OGSBURY

We developed novel exercise techniques to help the cubs overcome their bout with rickets.

DAVE KENNY

After being weighed, Snow examines her reflection in the microwave. DAVE KENNY

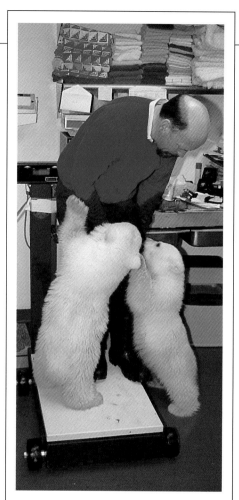

Only one at a time on the scale, please.
DAVE KENNY

Dr. Kenny says, "This is my coffee, Klondike." CANDY KANE

The cubs nurse with such force that both bottles have collapsed.

DAVE KENNY

Two hands just aren't enough to feed two hungry bears.

DAVE KENNY

Denny tries to convince Klondike that gruel tastes as good as milk.

CINDY BICKEL

You are supposed to lap the milk, not snort it up your nose.

DAVE KENNY

The cubs have graduated from bottle to bowl.

Klondike's bite is strong enough to dent a stainless steel bowl.
CINDY BICKEL

Snow's polar bear milk mustache.
DAVE KENNY

Being squirted with the hose was not one of the cubs' favorite activities.

JOHN EDWARDS

The cubs were outgrowing the wading pool.

CINDY BICKEL

The cubs quickly learned how to soak their keepers. CINDY BICKEL

Do you teach polar bears to swim?

The cubs relax on pillows of ice.

KATHY OGSBURY

KATHY OGSBURY

CANDY KANE

Armed now with teeth, Klondike guards his ice block. CANDY KANE

Growing up . . . on ice.

CINDY BICKEL

*Growing up . . .
with outside privileges.*

The cubs look bewildered on their first day outside the nursery. DAVE KENNY

*Eye to eye with
Dr. Kenny.*
CINDY BICKEL

Klondike is ready to protect his sister. CINDY BICKEL

Always together, Klondike and Snow. CINDY BICKEL

"Double Trouble!"

No shrub is safe from sampling. CINDY BICKEL

Snow emerges from under a tree. CINDY BICKEL

Juniper bushes—catnip for polar bears. CINDY BICKEL

Exploring the zoo in the late afternoon. CINDY BICKEL

Klondike wrestling with Dr. Kenny in the snow.
JOHN AMBROSE

Cubs go to Denny for a few minutes of comfort. As with human babies, sucking provides a sense of security.
CINDY BICKEL

With feet like snow shoes, the cubs can really "motor" in the snow.

DAVE KENNY

Stalking the tundra—Klondike explores the new-fallen snow.

DAVE KENNY

Klondike loves to roll in the snow, covering his face in white powder. DAVE KENNY

The snow is a
perfect place
for a polar
bear wrestling
match.

DAVE KENNY

The cubs seem
impervious to the
cold and snow of
Denver's winter.

DAVE KENNY

When scared, the cubs would run to their closest human parent for protection—in this case, surrogate mother Cindy.

DAVE KENNY

Bear Fever

Polar bears born in the wild are referred to by researchers as "Cubs of the Year" or "C.O.Y.'s." Klondike and Snow's popularity with the public and the media could deservedly garner them the title "Cubs of the Decade." When they were born, as wrinkled, not particularly cuddly babies, there was no way anyone could have predicted what celebrities they would become. Yes, they were uniquely adorable, but they didn't even resemble bears at birth. They looked more like wet, white hamsters than bears—so small and fragile that all their caretakers could hope for was their survival.

During those first few days, the line of visitors at the nursery window was typical of the number of people viewing any other zoo baby. No extraordinary procedures were taken to let the public see them. But, as Klondike and Snow grew, their appeal increased to a level unmatched in recent zoo history.

The bears are becoming a handful, even for the most dedicated zoo volunteers. CINDY BICKEL

The cubs spent much of their time watching visitors watch them.
CINDY BICKEL

Television stations were clamoring to get any news first—"Klondike and Snow survive their first week;" "The Denver Zoo's polar bear babies have opened their eyes;" "Klondike takes his first step;" . . . anything to bring this human interest story to the public. In Klondike and Snow's first four months of life, they were mentioned not less than 1100 times on national and even international television. As far away as Ecuador, London, Japan, and Holland, people were following their story.

Klondike and Snow stories were printed in newspapers around the world, even in a Japanese magazine! Associated Press articles prompted friends, relatives, and colleagues from other zoos to send clippings from their local papers—Los Angeles, Pittsburgh, and even Peoria! The people who were in charge of the babies' care became local celebrities for their valiant efforts—jobs for which they were trained and expected to do and yet, suddenly, applauded for.

With all this exposure it was only natural that the public wanted more. More meant hundreds of thousands of visitors streaming into the zoo at a record-breaking level with attendance soaring to 37 percent above the previous year—one that had been a record in itself. Hundreds of callers tied up the zoo's phone lines wishing the bears well, wanting assurance they were being properly cared for, requesting ways they could help. First graders, having learned of the cubs' earlier health problems, sent cards carefully written in crayon with words of comfort and concern: "we luv you, klondik and sno-get will sune." The zoo received many cards and letters from near and far. One even included a check for $8.01—the proceeds from three children's lemonade stand, offering to help offset the costs incurred in caring for the bears!

The zoo's gift shop sales of polar bear merchandise were unprecedented. A special polar bear tent was set up outside the nursery where people could purchase mementos of their visit with Klondike and Snow. An 800-number was established for the many national and international requests for Klondike and Snow memorabilia.

Snow and Klondike stuffed bears become a must for every young visitor. MEG KENNY

A panoramic view of visitors patiently waiting to see the bears. MEG KENNY

And with all the publicity, the lines to view the babies through the nursery window grew. After the first week, with the increase in polar bear watchers, it became necessary for zoo security and docents to quickly fill the gap in controlling the burgeoning crowds at the nursery. Amazingly, the line to the window moved along and no one felt slighted that, having waited twenty or more minutes, they were only allowed two or three minutes to view the small, white wonders. A ramp was built to accommodate two lines with children in front and adults on the raised platform. Hours went by and the expressions were always the same; awe, wonder, smiling faces. Voices buzzing with wistful comments about the experience were heard—

Klondike seems perplexed by the lack of response from a large stuffed bear. CINDY BICKEL

Kids and cubs—both fascinated with each other. JOHN EDWARDS

"how cute," "they look so cuddly," "how big they've grown," "Mom, can I take them home?". . . .

Everyone wanted to be part of this wonderful event.

The cubs drew smiles from even the youngest of visitors. KATHY OGSBURY

A plastic garbage can came in handy for exercising the cubs in the nursery. While Snow is strengthening her legs, Klondike is vying for attention. Cindy is dressed to ward off the formidable teeth and claws of the four-month-old cubs. CANDY KANE

A growing Klondike explores his new home. **DAVE KENNY**

Epilogue

The hidden life of the polar bear baby is one of nature's great and wonderful mysteries. In this respect, we and the public were given the rare opportunity to witness it—"up close and personal"—from Klondike and Snow's first moments of life.

We made the right decision that very first day to keep them in an incubator in the exhibit nursery and in full view of the public. This was an unprecedented event to be shared with everyone. As the cubs grew, the lines at the nursery also grew. They quickly became the most popular animals to have ever lived at the Denver Zoo. Klondike and Snow's dramatic fight for survival captured everyone's hearts.

The very fact that polar bears exist is a marvel of nature, one we should respect. Our plea to all who shared with us the joys of watching Klondike and

Dr. Kenny videotapes the swimming bears during their first "filled pool" swimming lesson.
MEG KENNY

Snow grow up is to insure that wild places are kept for all animals to carry out their lives as nature intended. In this way we will provide an inheritance for future generations that can't be bought or replaced.

From sucking on Denny's hands, to testing the waters in their temporary home, the bears mature into independence. DAVE KENNY, TOP

JOHN EDWARDS, BOTTOM

An airborne Snow does a polar bear belly flop into the pool.

KEN NEUBAUER

That polar bears exist is a marvel.

The profile of these wonderful animals makes their immense appeal easy to understand.

DAVE KENNY

Adjusting to their temporary home in the penguin exhibit, big brother Klondike goes first while Snow looks on. MARION EDWARDS

RIGHT: *In the water, the cubs play and splash—what could be more natural for polar bears!* DAVE KENNY

LEFT: *Klondike waits at the water's edge for Snow to emerge. When the ball comes between the two bears, Klondike first displays a dominant stance, then playfully pushes Snow—rough play but they keep coming back for more,* ABOVE. **DAVE KENNY**

Graduation from the zoo's hospital nursery—Cindy, Dave, and Denny, the cubs' best human friends, lead Klondike and Snow to their temporary exhibit. JACKIE ZEILER

On my final night with the cubs before they left the nursery permanently, I decided to sleep with them one last time. After the zoo closed, I moved the now five-month-old cubs to their new holding area. At 9 P.M., I returned to the bears with my air mattress and sleeping bag. Momentarily frightened, the cubs stood in a corner making bear faces and snorting at me.

As I set up my bed, they intently watched my every move. Once I was in the sleeping bag, Klondike slowly approached. He was intent on getting in the sleeping bag with me and sucking on any bare skin, as he did as a baby. I scolded him and pushed him out. He slowly circled the room, coming back to me while Snow watched, keeping her distance. I moved deeper into my sleeping bag thinking if Klondike couldn't see me, he would give up and go lie down with his sister. Not so. Every few minutes a large, hairy white face appeared in the sleeping bag a few inches from my face. He greeted me with a lick and tried to crawl inside. I thought he would tire and go to sleep, but he didn't. After about 30 minutes, I had to leave. It was at that moment that I knew that our close time together had ended. The cubs would have to leave their human family and I would no longer be an honorary member of the polar bear clan.

DAVID KENNY, V.M.D., SENIOR VETERINARIAN, DENVER ZOOLOGICAL GARDENS